I Like Being Me

Poems about kindness, friendship, and making good choices

Written by Judy Lalli

free spirit
PUBLISHING®

Library of Congress Cataloging-in-Publication Data
Names: Lalli, Judy, 1949– author.
Title: I like being me : poems about kindness, friendship, and making good choices / written by Judy Lalli.
Description: Golden Valley, MN : Free Spirit Publishing, [2016]
Identifiers: LCCN 2016002905 | ISBN 9781631980923 (paperback) | ISBN 1631980920 (soft cover) | ISBN 9781631981135 (Web PDF) | ISBN 9781631981142 (EPUB)
Subjects: LCSH: Identity—Juvenile poetry. | Self-esteem—Juvenile poetry. | Kindness—Juvenile poetry. | Children's poetry, American. | BISAC: JUVENILE NONFICTION / Poetry / General. | JUVENILE NONFICTION / Social Issues / Self-Esteem & Self-Reliance.
Classification: LCC PS3562.A412 A6 2016 | DDC 811/.54—dc23
LC record available at https://lccn.loc.gov/2016002905

Free Spirit Publishing does not have control over or assume responsibility for author or third-party websites and their content.

Reading Level 2; Interest Level Ages 4–8;
Fountas & Pinnell Guided Reading Level L

Edited by Marjorie Lisovskis and Alison Behnke
Cover and interior design and illustrations by Emily Dyer

Photo credits: pages iv, 5–6, 9, 13–14, 17–18, 21–22, 25, 33, 35, 38, 41–42, 45–46, 49–50 © Douglas Knutson; page 2 © YaoRusheng | Dreamstime.com; page 9 © Warangkana Charuyodhin | Dreamstime.com; pages 26, 37 © Wavebreakmedia Ltd | Dreamstime.com; page 29 © Nadezhda1906 | Dreamstime.com; page 30 © Emily Dyer; page 57 author photo © Joe Chielli

10 9 8 7 6 5 4
Printed in China
R18860821

Free Spirit Publishing Inc.
6325 Sandburg Road, Suite 100
Minneapolis, MN 55427-3674
(612) 338-2068
help4kids@freespirit.com
freespirit.com

FSC
www.fsc.org
MIX
Paper from responsible sources
FSC® C144853

Dedication

To Morris and Florence Goldsmith, my parents, who exposed me to the love of language and to the values expressed in these pages

To Diane O'Neill, who enthusiastically field-tested the poems with her students

To Doug Mason-Fry, whose creativity influenced me every step of the way

To Jim Botti, who encouraged me to persevere with the idea for this book

To Mary Martha Whitworth, who shared honest and caring feedback that enriched the project

And to Tony Lalli, who gave technical support to my writing and unconditional support to me

Contents

Dear Reader,

I think poems are fun. You can read them quietly to yourself or aloud to others. You can think about what they mean or just enjoy the sounds of the words. You can recite favorite poems over and over until they're a part of you and you know them by heart.

Photographs are fun, too. They can bring special meanings to words or give you new ideas. You can think about what's happening in a picture and wonder what might happen next. You can pretend that you're in a picture and imagine how you would feel.

I hope you enjoy the poems and photographs in this book. And I hope you like being you!

Love,

Judy Lalli

I Can Choose

I can choose
To win or lose.
I know it's up to me.

If I think that
I'm a winner,
That's what I will be!

I'm Waiting for a Rainbow

I'm waiting for a rainbow,
I'm waiting for the sun.
I'm waiting for the rain to stop
So I can play and run.

I know I should be patient,
But waiting's such a pain.
I guess I'll have to pass the time
Appreciating rain.

I Hear the Music Playing

I hear the music playing,
But I don't remember the song.

I hear the teacher talking,
But I get the directions wrong.

I hear the children reading,
But I miss where to follow along.

My hearing seems to be okay,
But my listening isn't strong.

I Didn't Believe I Could Do It

I didn't believe I could do it.
I was afraid to try.
My *teacher* believed I could do it,
And next time, so will I.

Mistakes Can Be Good

Mistakes can be good.
They can help you grow.
They can show you what you need to know.

So whenever you make a mistake,
Just say:
"Now I'll try another way."

At Least I'm Getting Better

I run and run and run and run,
And then I trip and fall.
I throw and catch and throw and catch,
And then I drop the ball.

I write my name and write my name,
And then I miss a letter.
But everybody makes mistakes.
At least I'm getting better!

13

Who Should I Be?

Who should I be on dress-up day?
I can wear a mask—
It's fun to play.

I can't decide who I should be,
Because most of the time
I like being me!

Broken Wagon

I'm mad.
It looks bad.
I think I broke my wagon.

It has a dent.
The wheel is bent.
And everything is draggin'.

The handle's loose.
Oh, what's the use?
I hope somebody kicks it.

I want to shout
And throw it out!
But I think I'd better fix it.

If I Promise to Do It

If I promise to do it,
I'll do it.

If I promise to go,
I'll be there.

If I promise to finish,
I'll finish.

Keeping my word
Shows I care.

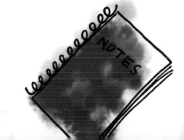

Don't Say "Crybaby!"

Don't say "Crybaby!"
Don't say "Dummy!"
Teasing makes me
Feel so crummy.

Falling down
Can bruise my knees,
But words can hurt
Where no one sees.

When I'm Cranky

When I'm cranky
I sass my mother,
I stamp my feet,
I boss my brother.

I think what I should do instead
Is jog,
Or jump,
Or go to bed.

I'm a Person, Too

I'm not as big as you,
But I'm a person, too.
So treat me with respect,
And that's how I'll treat you.

Someone Else's Chair

Want to learn about each other?
Want to show how much you care?
Just imagine what it's like
To sit in someone else's chair.

I Don't Have the Time

I don't have the time.
I don't really care.

I don't want to do it.
I don't think it's fair.

I don't want to help you.
Can't you understand?

WHOOPS! I slipped!
Will you give me a hand?

28

I Can't Move It

I can't move it,
You can't move it,
It won't move an inch.

But if we work together,
Moving it's a cinch.

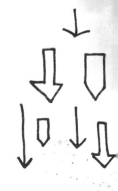

Hands

Hands can fight,
Hands can scare,
Or hands can join together
To show they care.

Someone Who Knows How to Share

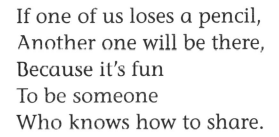

If one of us needs an eraser,
An eraser will be there,
Because it's fun
To be someone
Who knows how to share.

If one of us loses a pencil,
Another one will be there,
Because it's fun
To be someone
Who knows how to share.

And whenever we do something special,
We do it as a pair,
Because it's fun
To be someone
Who knows how to share.

I Hope You're As Lucky As I Am

I hope you have someone to play with,
Someone who cares what you say.
I hope you are always together—
Even if one goes away.

I hope you can share all your feelings,
I hope you don't have to pretend.
I hope you're as lucky as I am—
I hope someone calls you a friend.

36

Five Little People

Five little people began to play.

The first one said, "Do it my way!"
The second one said, "That's not fair!"
The third one said, "I don't care!"
The fourth one said, "This isn't fun!"
The fifth one said, "Our game is done!"

So five little people all walked away.
They never even got to play.

39

We're Telling the Teacher on You

"We're telling the teacher on you!"
"We're telling the teacher on you!"

Wait a minute! That's not fair!
The teacher wasn't even there.

She won't know what it's about.
So let's find ways to work it out.

I Forgot to Say "Please" and "Thank You"

I forgot to say "Please" and "Thank you."
I forgot to take turns with the ball.
I forgot to say "May I?" and "Sorry."
I forgot to use manners at all.

The other kids tried to remind me,
But I just forgot what to say.
Then *they* all forgot *their* manners—
They forgot to invite me to play.

There Are Only Two Kinds Of "I'm Sorry"

There are only two kinds of "I'm sorry,"
With no other kind in between.
There's the one that someone *tells* you to say,
And the one that you really mean.

You Can Use It

You can use it,
Reuse it,
Recycle it,
  and then
You can use it,
Reuse it, and
Recycle it again.

Or . . .

You can use it,
Abuse it,
Throw it on
  the ground,
Till all you see
  is trash
When you look
  around.

Or . . .

You can use it,
Reuse it,
Recycle it,
  and then
You can use it,
Reuse it, and
Recycle it again.

We Give Thanks

We give thanks
In late November.

But what about January
February
March
April
May
June
July
August
September
October
And December?

The best time for Thanksgiving
Is every day we're living.

Boring, Boring, Boring

Boring, boring, boring.
That's what my world would be
If everybody looked and talked
And acted just like me.

Discussion Starters and Activities

A Guide for Teachers, Families, and Other Caring Adults

I Like Being Me is a book of poems for children and the adults who care about them. We all know the power of poetry. We remember rhymes and songs that we learned long ago. Whether the messages are simple or profound, they can stick in our heads for years. Teachers, counselors, and family members can use this book to foster a love of poetry and teach social skills along the way. Children can listen to the poems, read them, memorize them, and recite them. They can discuss the poems, act them out, illustrate them, write about them, and use them as motivation for writing their own poems.

The poems in this book encourage children to understand that they have the power to make good choices. They can choose to have a positive attitude; they can choose to learn from their mistakes; they can choose to care, share, and cooperate.

Each poem focuses on at least one important theme or social skill, listed in the following chart. The poems at the beginning of the book deal with the choices children make for themselves, while the later poems deal with how children choose to interact with others. You can read the poems in order, or you might want to choose a poem and its related social skill whenever an opportunity for discussion arises. When you introduce a poem, you may choose to tell children what its theme is or ask for their thoughts and discuss their ideas.

Poems	Related Social Skills
"I Can Choose"	Having a positive attitude
"I'm Waiting for a Rainbow"	Being patient
"I Hear the Music Playing"	Listening
"I Didn't Believe I Could Do It"	Believing in yourself
"Mistakes Can Be Good"	Learning from mistakes
"At Least I'm Getting Better"	Persevering
"Who Should I Be?"	Liking yourself
"Broken Wagon"	Solving problems
"If I Promise to Do It"	Being dependable
"Don't Say 'Crybaby!'"	Being kind

Poems	Related Social Skills
"When I'm Cranky"	Dealing with feelings
"I'm a Person, Too"	Speaking up for yourself
"Someone Else's Chair"	Understanding others
"I Don't Have the Time"	Helping others
"I Can't Move It"	Cooperating
"Hands"	Making choices
"Someone Who Knows How to Share"	Sharing
"I Hope You're As Lucky As I Am"	Being a friend
"Five Little People"	Getting along
"We're Telling the Teacher on You"	Working it out
"I Forgot to Say 'Please' and 'Thank You'"	Being polite
"There Are Only Two Kinds of 'I'm Sorry'"	Apologizing
"You Can Use It"	Caring about our planet
"We Give Thanks"	Showing appreciation
"Boring, Boring, Boring"	Celebrating differences

Getting Started

- After choosing a poem, read it aloud a few times. Show children the photograph.

- Invite children to recite the poem with you. Depending on the children's age and ability level, you might recite a few words or lines with them and gradually encourage them to recite the poem on their own.

- Discuss the ideas in the poem. Ask children questions such as,

  » What choice did the person or people in this poem make? What might be some consequences of the choice? (If necessary, explain that consequences are results or effects that follow actions.) What other choices could the person or people have made?

  » Look at the photograph that goes with this poem. What do you think is happening in the picture? What do you think the person or people in the picture might be feeling or thinking?

  » When have you or people you know used the ideas or skills in this poem? (For example, think of times when someone learned from a mistake, had to be patient, or shared.) How did it feel to do this? Why can it sometimes be hard to make positive choices?

Building on the Book's Ideas

- When you want to get the group's attention, begin reciting a poem and encourage children to join in.

- When you notice someone behaving in a positive way mentioned in one of the poems, acknowledge the behavior by reciting or referring to the poem. ("You didn't believe you could do it!" or "You were being patient!" or "You're getting better!")

- Send home notes telling families about the themes of the poems. Invite parents to ask children to recite a poem from the book each week, and discuss the themes. Also ask families to share examples of their children using the social skills. (For instance, "Ariel shared with her sister," or "Juan persevered with his math homework," or, "We all learned from a mistake!")

- Connect poems with class procedures. For example, designate an area of the room as the "Work It Out" space, where children go to discuss disagreements as the children do in the poem "We're Telling the Teacher on You." Or create a "When I'm Cranky . . ." sign to post in your time-out area.

- The poems' themes lend themselves to connections with many wonderful pieces of literature. Gather books that emphasize similar ideas and read them—or have them available for children to read—to reinforce the social skills taught in the poems. For example, when discussing the idea of learning from mistakes, you could read *Regina's Big Mistake* by Marissa Moss, *Zach Makes Mistakes* by William Mulcahy, or *Beautiful Oops* by Barney Saltzberg.

Exploring Further

- Invite children to draw pictures reflecting the poems' ideas or to copy the poems into their notebooks and decorate the pages with designs and drawings.

- Have children write their own poems inspired by the poems in the book or write stories about themes from the poems.

- Invite children to clap along to the poems or to use movements to act them out. For example, for the poem "At Least I'm Getting Better," they could run in place, pretend to fall, mimic throwing a ball, and so on.

- Place children in small groups and assign a poem to each group. Have them develop simple skits demonstrating the main ideas in their poems.

- Plan a Poetry Festival. Each child or group of children can learn a poem and make simple "props on a stick" using colored poster board and dowels or rulers. They can hold these props while reciting the poem. (Children are often more comfortable speaking to a group when they have something to do with their hands.) The children can invite their families to the Poetry Festival or visit other classrooms to recite their poems.

- Have children work in groups to make posters inspired by the poems. They could write words or lines from their chosen poem, draw illustrations of the poems' ideas, or both.

- Invite adult guests to read poems from *I Like Being Me* and other favorite poems. Afterword, facilitate a discussion about the poems that the visitors have read. Often, visitors share wonderful stories about the poems they learned as children or why certain poems have had an impact on them.

A Final Word

I hope that you and all of my readers enjoy these poems and their rhymes, rhythms, and messages. I'd love to hear about the ways in which you share this book with the children who matter in your life. Please feel free to write to me in care of my publisher at help4kids@freespirit.com. I look forward to hearing from you!

—Judy Lalli

Acknowledgments

I am so excited about this updated edition of *I Like Being Me,* and I am grateful for all of the work that went into its creation. I also want to acknowledge with gratitude my students who were the first "editors" of the original edition. They read, recited, and discussed each new poem as I wrote it. They suggested changes if the words didn't flow or the rhymes seemed forced. And when I wondered whether my readers would understand the message I was trying to convey in each poem, my students reassured me and reminded me how much children are capable of understanding. I appreciate learning that lesson from them.

About the Author

Judy Lalli is the coordinator of online learning for PLS 3rd Learning after having enjoyed a wonderful career as a classroom teacher in Norristown, Pennsylvania. She holds B.S. and M.S. degrees from the University of Pennsylvania, and she has also completed extensive postgraduate work. Judy is a visiting author to classrooms around the country, and she is a recipient of the Delaware Valley Reading Association's Celebrate Literacy Award for her work promoting early literacy development.

Illustrator

Emily Dyer is a designer at Free Spirit Publishing, as well as for a variety of freelance clients. Her licensed illustration work can be found on products ranging from greeting cards to textiles. She lives in Minneapolis with her husband, two sons, a Cairn Terrier named Waffles, and a hound-mix named Sal.

Photographer

Doug Knutson is a Minneapolis-based people photographer working for a wide variety of publishers, magazines, corporations, and advertising agencies. Assignments have taken him across the United States and around the world. As part of a personal project, Knutson has photographed twenty-two Nobel Peace Laureates.

More Great Books from Free Spirit

I'm Like You, You're Like Me
A Book About Understanding and
Appreciating Each Other
by Cindy Gainer, illustrated by Miki Sakamoto
48 pp., color illust., PB & HC, 11¼" x 9¼", ages 3–8.

F Is for Feelings
by Goldie Miller and Lisa A. Berger,
illustrated by Hazel Mitchell
40 pp., color illust., PB, 11¼" x 9¼", ages 3–8.

We Can Get Along
A Child's Book of Choices
by Lauren Murphy Payne,
illustrated by Melissa Iwai
40 pp., color illust., PB & HC, 11¼" x 9¼", ages 3–8.

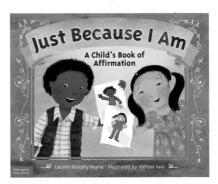

Just Because I Am
A Child's Book of Affirmation
by Lauren Murphy Payne,
illustrated by Melissa Iwai
36 pp., color illust., PB & HC, 11¼" x 9¼", ages 3–8.

Interested in purchasing multiple quantities and receiving volume discounts?
Contact edsales@freespirit.com or call 1.800.735.7323 and ask for Education Sales.

Many Free Spirit authors are available for speaking engagements, workshops, and keynotes.
Contact speakers@freespirit.com or call 1.800.735.7323.

For pricing information, to place an order, or to request a free catalog, contact:

free spirit PUBLISHING®

6325 Sandburg Road • Suite 100 • Minneapolis, MN 55427-3674
toll-free 800.735.7323 • local 612.338.2068 • fax 612.337.5050
help4kids@freespirit.com • freespirit.com